The
Goffins
Togas and Treasure

The Goffins

Togas and Treasure

JEANNE WILLIS

illustrated by **Nick Maland**

**WALKER
BOOKS**

For Judy Owens. Much love
J.W.

For David and Maddy with love
N.M.

First published 2011 by Walker Books Ltd
87 Vauxhall Walk, London SE11 5HJ

2 4 6 8 10 9 7 5 3 1

Text © 2011 Jeanne Willis
Illustrations © 2011 Nick Maland

The right of Jeanne Willis and Nick Maland to be identified as
author and illustrator respectively of this work has been asserted by them
in accordance with the Copyright, Designs and Patents Act 1988

This book has been typeset in ITC Veljovic

Printed and bound in Great Britain by Clays Ltd, St Ives plc

British Library Cataloguing in Publication Data:
a catalogue record for this book is available from the British Library

ISBN 978-1-4063-0872-3

www.walker.co.uk

CONTENTS

THE CARRUTHERS

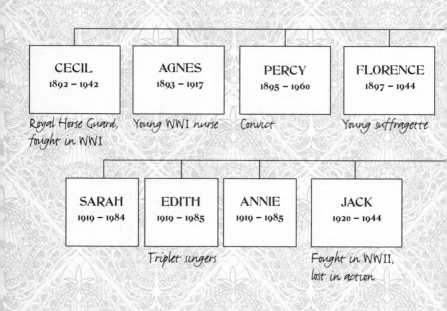

CECIL
1892 – 1942

Royal Horse Guard,
fought in WWI

AGNES
1893 – 1917

Young WWI nurse

PERCY
1895 – 1960

Convict

FLORENCE
1897 – 1944

Young suffragette

SARAH
1919 – 1984

EDITH
1919 – 1985

ANNIE
1919 – 1985

Triplet singers

JACK
1920 – 1944

Fought in WWII,
lost in action

FAMILY TREE

MONTAGUE CARRUTHERS
1870 – 1960
m
MAUD GOODWIN
1871 – 1971

Explorer, sailor, whaling ship

Suffragette, Titanic, WWI Nurse, maid servant called Violet, lived to be 100

SID
1899 – 1975
m
DOLLY GRAY
1900 – 1975

Joined army to fight WWI, under age, lost leg, won medals

VICTORIA
1901 – 1904

GORDON
1922 – 2005
m
PEGGY ELLIS
1926 –

Fought against Hitler in WWII as a young man

MARY
1926 – 2006

Evacuee

FRANK
1928 – 2003

Evacuee

SIMON
1958 –

PHILLIP
1960 –
m
SUSAN DERBYSHIRE
1966 –

Saved child from drowning

GEORGE
1999 –

Discovered Goffins living in his grandma's attic

CHAPTER ONE

PUNCTURES AND POST BOXES

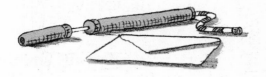

"Oh, Rex! Now look what you've done," groaned George.

Ever since he'd given Rex a home, the pup seemed to be chewing his way out of it. He'd already eaten through the side of his basket, swallowed a slipper and nibbled the tassels off Grandma Peggy's curtains. Now he'd sunk his miniature fangs into George's bicycle tyre.

George sighed as he got down on his hands and knees to fix the puncture, but he could never stay cross with Rex for long, even when he'd damaged his beloved BMX.

Togas and Treasure

His friend Jermaine from back in London had been the first to get a BMX. The stunts he could do on that bike were the talk of Hazelwood Junior School. He made it look so easy, but when George got the same bike and tried to copy Jermaine by pedalling headfirst down the highest slide in the park, he realized, sometime before the ambulance arrived, that doing stunts was much harder than it looked.

Luckily, he'd only bumped his head but, as his mother kept reminding him, he could have broken his neck and ended up in a wheelchair. She was a nurse and knew these things. After the accident, George's mum had banned him from riding his BMX, but now they were living with Grandma Peggy, the ban had been lifted so he could cycle to his new school. If George didn't manage to fix the tyre this weekend, he'd have to get the bus to school, and that would mean getting up a lot earlier than he liked.

As George tried to wrestle the end of the bicycle pump from Rex's sharp little teeth, he felt as if he was being watched, and cast his eyes up to the roof top. Sure enough, the Goffins were looking down. Lofty was leaning dangerously over the edge while Eave tended the plants growing around the chimney pot. She put down the antique copper kettle she used as a watering can and gave George a cheery wave. In that split second, he forgot himself and waved back.

"Who are you waving to, boy?" asked Grandma Peggy.

George whipped round. Grandma had come through the French windows of her bedsit, which opened onto the garden. She jabbed her walking stick towards the sky.

"Yoo hoo! Who's up there?"

11

George laughed nervously. "Nobody, Grandma. Don't be daft."

Grandma Peggy fixed him with a steely stare. "I'm not as daft as I look, boy," she said. "Not by a long chalk."

That was certainly true. Since George discovered Lofty and Eave living secretly in Grandma Peggy's attic, he had a sneaking suspicion she knew they were there all along. If not, why would she insist that all her meals were brought to her on a basket with a fancy handle? George was convinced it was so she could put her leftovers out in the basket and Lofty could hook it up with his fishing rod; George had seen it happen! Grandma insisted the food was for the birds, but did birds eat spaghetti? Or sausages? George didn't think so, but he knew two people in the attic who did.

For generations, refugees from the sunken island of Inish Goff had been living in the tops of abandoned buildings and belfries across the land, unbeknownst to Them Below. Lofty had told George that no matter where he lived, he was never more than five roofs away from a Goffin.

George never ceased to be amazed at how Lofty and Eave managed to survive on so little, but the more he got to know them, the more he saw that Goffins were very practical people. Lofty and Eave had sorted and recycled everything around them, turning the loft into a little palace, using old furniture and junk that his ancestors had stored there, going right back to his great-great-grandparents.

Grandma gave George's floppy tyre a prod.

"Looks like your inner tube's gone, boy. How d'you do that, then?"

"I didn't do it. Rex did," said George.

"Ouf!" said Grandma. "Don't you go blaming him. It's your fault for teasing him, making the wheels go round and round like that and getting him all excited."

13

It seemed Rex could do no wrong in Grandma's eyes. George might have taken offence at the way she always sided with the dog, but if it hadn't been for her, his dad wouldn't have let him keep Rex in the first place. He was grateful to Grandma for that. He'd even grown to love her grumpiness – it made him laugh.

"Never mind laughing," said Grandma, waving an envelope at him. "Are you going to post this letter for me or not? Only I can't get to the post box. Not with my legs."

It was quite a long way to the post box and George didn't fancy going on foot, what with it being Saturday, and what with him being a bit lazy.

"Do I have to, Grandma?" he moaned. "Only my bike's bust, and anyway, I've got to do my project about the Romans for school."

The minute the words slipped out of his mouth, he knew he'd said the wrong thing. Eave would have been furious if she'd heard him talk to his grandma like that. The Goffin way was to respect their elders and to do a Kindness without being asked. Even Rex seemed to look shocked, lying on the floor with his paws over his eyes.

"You don't have to go, no," said Grandma, whose face had gone a strange shade of purple. "But if you can't even walk to the post box and do a bit of homework when your Grandpa Gordon managed to march 200 miles on an empty stomach to defeat the Nazis, I feel sorry for you."

George didn't want to hear it, but he knew Grandma was right. He came from a long line of heroic men on his father's side. Grandpa Gordon had won a medal in World War II.

Togas and Treasure

Great-Grandpa Sid had fought in World War I and Great-Great-Grandpa Montague had explored half the world, travelling in appalling conditions, fighting off wild beasts, pirates and hostile natives at every turn. He knew all this because Eave had found the medals, diaries, letters and an almanac in the loft and pieced together their life stories. She'd even drawn up a family tree.

Being the last-born child, George was at the bottom of his family tree, but that didn't mean he had to be the lowest of the low. He stood up, put his shoulders back and took Grandma's envelope.

"I'll post it," he said.

"I should hope so," she grumbled. "It's a letter of complaint. I sent off for something special and they promised to deliver it last week, only they haven't and it's not good enough."

George was intrigued. "How special? What have you bought?"

Grandma tapped her nose. "Can't tell you anything except it's big, red and shiny. Keep it under your hat – if your dad finds out I've ordered it, he won't want me to have it and he'll try to stop me."

George's mind was boggling. "Cool ... is it a motorbike?"

Grandma felt in her dressing gown pocket and pulled out a crumpled ten pound note.

"Never you mind," she said. "Here, buy yourself a new inner tube."

George said thanks, stuffed the letter and the money in the pocket of his hoodie and went indoors, Rex trotting at his heels. He was in half a mind to ask his dad for a lift but he always had a lie-in at the weekend and, anyway, Grandma's words were still ringing in his head about Grandpa Gordon marching all that way on an empty stomach. If he grabbed a handful of chocolate digestives, he could probably make it to the shops and post box without fainting from exhaustion.

Togas and Treasure

Given that his mum was at work, it was the perfect opportunity to raid the fridge to top up the Goffins' food supply. Eave's pet pigeon, Chimbley, provided them with plenty of eggs and there was honey from the wild bees who'd made their home behind a hole in the plaster, but they never had any butter, so he cut the end off the pack and put it in a plastic bag along with the end of a cucumber, some yogurt that was just past its sell-by date, and a half-finished bottle of dandelion and burdock. If they needed anything else, he could pick it up from the shops.

He went up the three flights of stairs to his bedroom and knocked on the small, green door opposite the end of his bed, using the agreed code.

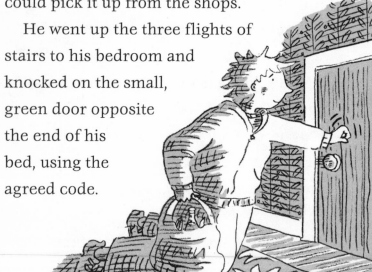

Pom ... tiddy pom pom ... pom pom!

He heard familiar soft footsteps as Eave approached. She flung open the door, her gooseberry-green eyes wild with excitement. She was waving a miniature letter at him.

"Jowge! Yourself will never be guessin' who's comin' to see us!"

Chapter Two

ROAMINS AND RUINS

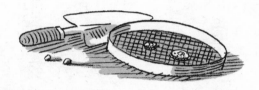

George took the letter from Eave.

"Did Chimbley bring it?" he asked.

Eave nodded so hard, the silk bows flew off the end of her wiry, copper plaits. "Herself be bringin' it just afore sunrise. 'Tis from myne muppy Ariel!"

The writing was tiny. George held it up to the chandelier that hung from the rafters but it was impossible for him to read Eave's mum's handwriting in the shadows of the candlelit attic, even if he screwed up his eyes.

"Yourself be needin' goggils, Jowge Carruthers," tutted Eave, grabbing the letter back. "Shall myneself be tellin' you what it says?"

Just then, Lofty appeared out of the gloom with a can of engine oil. Quite a lot of it had gone down the front of the voluminous Victorian sailor's trousers he'd chosen to wear.

"Mornin' Jowge. Goodly news about myne oh-nee son Arch a-comin' to visit, yay?"

"You're kidding! Arch is actually coming here – to this house?" said George. "Wow!"

Eave threw her hands in the air and screwed up her face. "Pappy! Myneself be rarin' to tell Jowge about myne brother Arch! How darst yourself be blurtin' it out and spoilin' myne besterly surprise?"

She threw herself onto the battered old chaise longue in the part of the attic they'd turned into a sitting room and beat her fists on the tapestry cushion. If any other girl had thrown a fit like that, George would have found it annoying. But when Eave did it, he just wanted to comfort her. She insisted she was nine, but she was no bigger than a five year old and he couldn't help feeling protective towards her. She was, after all, the little sister he'd always wanted; his step-in sister, or so she called herself. George sat down next to her.

"Hey ... Eave." He prodded her playfully in the ribs. "OK, so I know Arch is coming now, but I still don't know why – that has to be the best bit of the surprise."

"Aha!" said Lofty, butting in enthusiastically. "Himself be a-comin' because..."

Eave threw the cushion at him. "Pappy, shush! Myneself be tellin' this news to Jowge!"

Whatever the news was, it had to be really important. Lofty and Eave were falling over themselves to tell George why, after more than two years, Arch was daring to leave the church belfry where he lived with his grandmother and mother, to visit them. Had the worst thing that could ever happen to a Goffin happened: had they been discovered?

"Nay, but themselves soon will be!" insisted Eave. "The olden-day diggers be arrivin'."

"The olden-day diggers?" George didn't understand.

"Yay, somebiddy be findin' ancient Roamin munnee Down Below and now the olden-day diggers be siftin' the soil lookin' for trove."

"Oh!" exclaimed George. "You mean archaeologists? They've actually found Roman remains outside the ruined church where your Granny Cloister lives?"

He'd been learning about the Romans at school and was supposed to have handed in his project last week. So far, he hadn't felt the slightest bit inspired but the idea that Eave's closest relatives were living on top of a pile of ancient Roman treasure suddenly brought the whole subject alive.

"Maybe there are gold goblets! Jewel-encrusted swords!" he enthused.

"Yay, and maybe myne fambily will be cotched if themselves doesn't flee most swiftlee," said Eave, wringing her over-sized frilly apron.

This was a deadly serious situation. It was bad enough that Eave and Lofty had to live apart from the rest of their family in the first place, but Granny Cloister needed looking after and there wasn't enough room for them all to live in the belfry together. But where would Ariel, Arch and Granny Cloister live, now that they had to leave? There were precious few places left in the country where three Goffins could survive in secret. Eave tapped the letter and smiled a small, hopeful smile.

"Myne Great-Uncool Garret be offerin' to put them up. Himself be livin' aloft in a windymill by his lonesome. Darst say there be room to spare..."

"Garret be doin' myne fambily a normous Kindness," interrupted Lofty. "Oh-nee 'tis too far to the windymill for Granny Cloister to be hobblin'."

George suspected as much. When Goffins travelled it had to be on foot under the cover of darkness and Granny Cloister was very old – 104, if he remembered rightly. Not surprisingly, her legs weren't what they used to be. She'd never make it and, despite Eave constantly reminding him that her brother was ox-strong, George doubted that even Arch could carry his granny all that way on his back.

"We need ... a plan," he said, struggling to think of one.

Lofty waved his oil can triumphantly. "Us has a plan, Jowge!"

"A grandlee plan!" agreed Eave. "Come see."

She led him out of the parlour, past the
painted portraits of his ancestors, along
the corridor of antique mirrors and past
her bedroom. They turned left at the little
bathroom hidden behind its curtain of plastic
macs, then took a sharp right until they came
to an erected canvas tent that had clearly
seen better days. The original pole that held it
up had been replaced by a pogo stick and the
door flaps looked as if they'd been slashed
by huge claws.

Togas and Treasure

"Don't tell me, it used to belong to Great-Great-Grandpa Montague!" laughed George.

"'Tis the same tent himself did sleep in whilst explorin' the Nile," said Lofty. "And now? 'Tis myne workshop."

He undid the flaps and, with a flourish, invited George to crawl inside. In the middle of the tent, surrounded by oily rags and an assortment of nuts, bolts, cogs and chains, was a small but beautifully constructed vehicle – a bit like a go-cart, only much better.

"'Tis a Goff-cart," announced Lofty.

"Wow!" said George. "It's brilliant!"

"Pappy did make it," said Eave proudly, crawling in behind him. "Myneself did send a letter to Arch, sayin' 'twas fixed. Himself be fetchin' it from Down Below come midnight."

Togas and Treasure

George rocked back on his heels and admired Lofty's handiwork. The back wheels had come from a big old-fashioned pram, as had the brake and the hood. The adjustable steering column had once been part of a child's scooter; George wondered if it had belonged to his dad. It was the seat that impressed him most though: it looked like a miniature throne, complete with a heavily-padded, buttoned back and braided armrests.

"Darst say 'tis from the Orient," said Lofty, patting the seat. "Grandmuppy Cloister will be findin' it most comftible on ye old botticks, yay?"

"For shame!" giggled Eave. "Pappy, yourself must not be speakin' of botticks. Whatever must Jowge be thinkin'?"

But all George was thinking was how much he wanted to take the Goff-cart for a ride.

"Shall I take it for a test-drive?" he asked. "I've got to post a letter for Grandma Peggy so I could take it up to the shops."

Lofty took out a spanner and adjusted the bolts on the front wheel.

"Thanklee, Jowge. 'Tis as well to give itself a run."

George couldn't believe his luck. But then his face fell. How on earth would they get it out of the attic? He was sure the stairs were too steep and, anyway, what if his dad came out of the bedroom and caught him bumping it down? Happily, Lofty had it all under control.

31

"When the coast be clear, myneself and Littley be lowerin' it out of the sky-like."

"On chains an' pulleys," added Eave.

It was all sorted. Lofty and Eave would lower the Goff-cart out of the attic window and down the side of the house, where George would be waiting in secret to drive it away.

"Do you need a hand getting it onto the roof?" he asked.

As soon as the words were out of his mouth, he regretted it. No matter how many times he'd climbed out of the attic window to join Eave in the roof garden, he still hadn't conquered his fear of heights. To his great relief, Lofty insisted they could manage without him. George had one last thought before he left.

"Do you need anything from the shops?" he asked.

Lofty shook his head. "Nay thanklee, Jowge. Us isn't needin' anythin'..."

"Exceptin' maybe some biskies," added Eave.

"And maybe some meatypaste," continued Lofty.

"And maybe a ninny goat," said Eave. "Then us could be milkin' herself."

"I'm afraid they don't sell goats at our shops," grinned George. "But I'll get Arch some sweets, shall I?"

Eave did a shimmy of excitement. "Yay, Arch be likin' sweets! Oh, myneself is burstin' to see myne oh-nee brother!"

After everything she'd told him, George could hardly wait to meet him either.

CHAPTER THREE

CARTS AND CRASHES

George waited round the side of the house with Rex and held his breath as Lofty and Eave lowered the Goff-cart over the edge of the roof. What if the chain snapped? What if the cart plummeted and crushed him? Even worse, what if somebody saw?

He should have had more faith in the Goffins. Lofty was far too clever not to check the chain was oiled and although he was very short for a man, he was as strong as two. And Eave would never have let her Pappy do anything that put her step-in brother at risk.

As it happened, only George witnessed the Goff-cart coming down, as smoothly and silently as if it was floating. He unhooked the chains, gave Eave the thumbs-up and watched her wind them back up. George wished she wouldn't stand so close to the edge, but she was sky-savvy: she was perfectly at home leaping about among the chimney pots.

George pushed the Goff-cart away from the house and onto the pavement, then sat down on the luxurious padded seat with Rex squashed in by his side, and pedalled like fury until he was out of sight.

He got some very strange glances as he steered his way to the shops, but he took them to be looks of admiration. How could anyone *not* be impressed by this vehicle? He wished his old friends could see him

now – especially Jermaine. He would have
been highly impressed by the speeds it
could reach going down even the smallest
slope and, quite frankly, it made the stunt
bikes look rather sluggish.

George came to an
impressive skid outside the
post office, dismounted and posted
Grandma's letter of complaint in the post
box. He was reluctant to leave the cart
unattended, but he didn't think Mr Shah
would be too pleased if he took it into his
grocery shop, so he left Rex to guard it.

"If anyone tries to nick it, bark!" he said.
"Lofty will never forgive me if anything
happens to it."

George went inside and picked up a pot of beef paste, a packet of assorted biscuits from the bargain bin, a sherbet fountain for Arch and a bag of jelly babies for Eave. As he went to pay, he remembered her last request and smiled at the shopkeeper.

"I don't suppose you sell goats, do you, Mr Shah?"

To his surprise, Mr Shah waved his hand in the direction of the stationery aisle.

"I have a small selection of waterproof mackintoshes over by the party poppers."

"Not coats, *goats*," grinned George. "Never mind, doesn't matter."

"Goats?" said Mr Shah. "Sadly no. I sell stamps and general items only."

He might well have stocked goats though – he sold just about everything else: bottles of bubbles, pipe racks, passport holders. Light bulbs. Raincoats. Jigsaw puzzles. And there were kittens for sale in the window.

"Do you sell inner tubes?" asked George.

"An inner tube is not a general item," insisted Mr Shah. "What you want to do is go to the bicycle shop in Rigby Street – Wheel Meet Again."

"Will we?" said George.

"That is the name of the shop," explained Mr Shah, rolling his eyes. "Wheel Meet Again. It's up the hill."

He wasn't wrong there. What's more, it was a very steep hill. It was impossible to pedal the Goff-cart up to Wheel Meet Again, so George had to push it. By the time he got there, he was red in the face. Once again, Rex was put on guard.

Togas and Treasure

"Remember," said George, "if anyone comes near, bark your head off, OK?"

"Arf! Arf! ARF!" barked Rex, obediently.

"I meant anyone except me," sighed George.

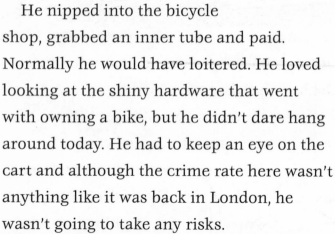

He nipped into the bicycle shop, grabbed an inner tube and paid. Normally he would have loitered. He loved looking at the shiny hardware that went with owning a bike, but he didn't dare hang around today. He had to keep an eye on the cart and although the crime rate here wasn't anything like it was back in London, he wasn't going to take any risks.

He climbed back into the seat next to Rex, stuffed the shopping in the cavity underneath and set off down the hill with the wind blowing into his hoody like a windsock.

Several people had to jump out of the way and although he apologized profusely,

it was too late for them to hear it because he had already gone whistling by.

As he shot back past Mr Shah's Post Office and Grocery Store, the speed certainly

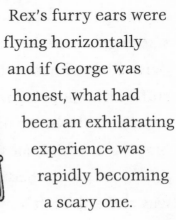

seemed to be picking up. Rex's furry ears were flying horizontally and if George was honest, what had been an exhilarating experience was rapidly becoming a scary one.

41

As he whizzed across the main road, George mistook Rex's tail for the brake and grabbed it. Rex whipped around and nipped him, pulling George's steering off-course and as the cart rocketed round the corner, George realized

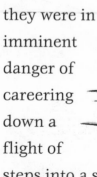

they were in imminent danger of careering down a flight of

steps into a sunken flowerbed in front of the Town Hall. He stuck his foot out sideways to try and stop the cart – but to no avail.

As the smell of burning trainer rubber filled his nostrils, George stuck out his other foot, praying that the whole contraption

would come to a halt, but it was too late.
There was a horrible sound of metal scraping
concrete as the cart clipped the top step,
pivoted and juddered all the way down,
finally flipping over in the petunias with
George and Rex beneath it and flinging the
shopping in all directions.

It was a miracle neither of them were
hurt, which is more than could be said for
the Goff-cart. It was in bits – springs were
hanging out of the seat, the brake cable was
severed, and the back wheel had folded in
half like an omelette. George put his head
in his hands and swore.

It took ages to limp back home with the cart, not least because his knee really hurt where he'd landed on it. By the time he'd got it back into Grandma Peggy's garden, George felt close to tears. He refused to cry though. He bet Arch never cried.

"Blimey. What happened to you?" said his dad, who was picking dog mess off the lawn with a plastic scoop. He waved a purple bag of poo at George. "Your job, I believe?" he said.

George was usually very good at clearing up after Rex but he'd forgotten to do it this morning – he'd had a great deal on his mind, after all.

"My fault," muttered Grandma, in George's defence. "I sent him to post a letter."

Grandma was sitting in her wheelchair by the French windows. She didn't mind sitting in it in private, but she refused to be seen in it in public.

"Nice wheels, boy," she said. "What happened? Did you drive it off a bridge?"

"Brakes failed," mumbled George, rubbing his knee.

His dad put the pooper scooper down and bounded over to have a proper look at the crashed cart. He seemed impressed. Despite the terrible damage, it was plain to see that the cart had real class.

"Who made this?" he asked, fingering the ripped upholstery on the seat.

"Loft ... hausen," lied George. "My friend from school ... Hans Lofthausen. His dad made it for him. He's German."

"I can tell by the engineering," said his dad, in all seriousness.

"We have to fix it," pleaded George. "Or Mr Lofthausen will kill me."

45

Togas and Treasure

George's father sprang into action. Since knowing Lofty and Eave, George had seen, to his surprise, that it was possible for a child to enjoy spending time with their parents. He'd grown much closer to his dad recently, which was great, but occasionally his dad got a bit over-keen – like now.

"Right! Let me have a look at it," he said. "George, fetch my spanner. I can fix the brake, no problem. Straighten the axle. What we really need though is a new wheel."

To George's horror, his father looked up at the roof.

"I bet there's a spare wheel in the attic," he said. "This bent one looks like a pram wheel. I bet there's an old pram up there somewhere among the junk, isn't there, Mum?"

He directed this question at Grandma Peggy.

"A pram? No, son," she said. "I think Gordon cleared everything out."

George's dad pulled a face. "Dad never threw anything away," he said. "It used to drive you mad, remember? I'll go and have a look."

Grandma struggled out of her wheelchair. "Here, have the wheels off this old clap-trap," she said. "I hate the thing. I don't know why you made me buy it, Phillip. I never wanted it."

But he'd already turned to go inside. It was too late to warn Lofty and Eave – unless George could think of a way to stop him, his dad would go up into the loft and discover them. With a thumping heart, he tried to call his father back.

"Dad! Forget it, Mr Lofthausen won't really kill me…"

George shot a desperate look at Grandma. If she knew about the Goffins as he suspected, if she really cared, she'd do something. But she was just standing there.

Togas and Treasure

No she wasn't ... she was
wobbling! First she
tottered to the left, then
she tottered to the right,
then very carefully,
holding onto the wall
of the raised flowerbed,

she bent her cranky knees
and sank very gingerly onto
her bottom. It all happened
in such slow-motion
and looked so comical,
George just stood and
watched with his mouth
hanging open.

"Grandma ... what the...?"

She rolled onto her side, smoothed
her skirt to make sure her
petticoat wasn't showing,
then began to yell for
all she was worth.

"Help! I've fallen!"

It was a fine piece of acting – or was it?
George couldn't quite tell.

"Fetch your dad. Hurry up," she muttered
through her teeth, then she clutched at her
heart and began yelling again.

"Help! Phil...lip! I've fallen!"

Rex, utterly convinced that Grandma Peggy
was about to peg it, threw back his head and
began to howl like a small wolf. George ran
indoors and bellowed up the stairs.

"Dad! Come quick! Grandma's broken both
her legs!"

CHAPTER FOUR

INJURIES AND OINTMENT

As it turned out, Grandma's injuries appeared to be minimal – her legs weren't bruised, let alone broken. She hadn't even laddered her tights. Even so, the ambulance crew insisted on taking her to hospital just to be on the safe side.

"You can't be too careful with the elderly," they said, wheeling her up the ramp into the ambulance.

"I'm not deaf and I'm not elderly!" snapped Grandma.

She was only deaf when she chose to be, it seemed, and although she was born in 1926, she didn't like to think of herself as an old person, even if she couldn't manage on her own these days. George's dad fussed with the blanket that had been placed over Grandma Peggy's knees.

"I'm coming with you, mum," he insisted.

"Shall I come too?" asked George.

He quite fancied a ride in an ambulance, especially if they put the sirens on, but Grandma clearly didn't want him there.

"No, I've got enough people gawping at me, boy. Get on with your day," she said. She waved her hand at him wearily and started to complain loudly about a pain in her hip.

"Hurry up... Ooh, I bet I've cracked my pelvis. My cousin Ida had that happen to her and she never rode a horse again."

George noticed that her light blue eyes were twinkling as if she was trying not to laugh. Had she had a real fall? Maybe old ladies always fell in slow motion. Or had she deliberately created this drama to cause a diversion? George could never be quite certain with Grandma.

"Get well soon, Grandma!" he waved, as the ambulance doors closed behind her.

The ambulance drove off, leaving George to face the miserable task of confessing to Lofty and Eave about the smashed-up cart. He picked up the shopping and went back into the house, dreading every step on the three flights of stairs that brought him closer to the attic. He knocked on the small, green door.

Pom ... tiddy pom pom ... pom pom!

When Lofty let him in, it was obvious from his expression that he already knew what had happened. Doubtless he'd looked over the edge of the roof and seen his handiwork in pieces Down Below. He looked disappointed rather than angry, which made George feel even worse. He hung his head.

"I'm so sorry, Lofty."

"Nay, Jowge. *Myneself* must be sayin' sorry for usin' such rickety brakes. For shame! Yourself could have been deaded."

Lofty hid his face in his hands. George put a reassuring arm around him.

"I'm OK," he said. "Really. I just grazed my knee. I'm not even sure the crash was anything to do with the brakes." He didn't think it was right for Lofty to take the blame. "It was a combination of things," continued George. "Hills and obstacles, mostly. People standing in the way and ... um ... Rex kind of sitting on the controls."

Lofty peered up at him from under his bushy, flame-red fringe, which looked as if it had exploded out of his head rather than grown.

"Us must be lookin' on the bright side, yay?" he ventured. "Yourself did bravelee test myne cart afore Grandmuppy Cloister, thus savin' herself from a most terribil accibump."

Lofty shook George warmly by the hand, then his eyes filled with fresh concern.

"Jowge, whatfor be happenin' to Grandmuppy Peg? Us be seein' herself gettin' into the amberlance, a-hollerin' and a-skrikin'."

"Don't you worry about her," smiled George. "She had a very small fall. It was more of a sit-down, really. She'll be fine. She's as tough as old boots."

Just then, Eave came bumbling out of the darkness wearing a nurse's cap and threatened George with a tube of ointment. George knew both items had once belonged to his Great-Great-Grandma's daughter, Agnes; some time ago, Eave had shown him the old medical kit and the medal Agnes had been given for saving so many soldiers.

"Jowge Carruthers! Be showin' Nurse Eave your sorely knee!" she insisted, dragging him by the hand and forcing him to sit down on the battered chaise longue. He rolled up the left leg of his tracksuit bottoms. There was a nasty graze and the skin was already turning a violent shade of green. Eave rubbed it with the ointment, which stank.

"Ow!" grumbled George. "It stings!"

"Yourself is bein' such a normous bubby!" said Eave briskly.

George gritted his teeth and tried not to wince. No doubt 'lionbrave' Arch would remain strong and silent even if somebody cut his head off.

"Oh no... Arch!" remembered George. "He'll be outside expecting to pick up the Goff-cart tonight, won't he? Shouldn't we get in touch with him?"

"'Tis too late to be tellin' himself not to come now," admitted Lofty. "No use sendin' a Chimbley note to yonder belfry neither – myne fambily be long-gone, for fear of bein' cotched by the olden-day diggers. Themselves be in hidin' for now."

"But where will they hide?" asked George. "It's still light. Goffins can't travel until after dark, can they?" He was worried sick about them now.

"Darst say Arch did take 'em into the church cellar and through the spewer pipe, which be leadin' to the wilde woods," explained Lofty. "'Tis the oh-nee escape route."

"Spewer pipe be most ponky," added Eave, wrinkling her freckled nose as if there was a bad smell under it. "Themselves will be gaggin' to get to Great-Uncool Garret's. Howfor will they be travellin' now, Pappy? Can yourself be fixin' the cart?"

Lofty frowned. "'Tis doubtfil us can be hoistin' it back onto the roof. And even supposin' myneself be mendin' it anew, howfor can us be knowin' 'tis safe? Darst not risk it, Littley."

Eave's gooseberry-green eyes filled with tears. "Myneself be – uff – uff – so afrit for myne fambily!" she sniffed, dabbing at her tears with the corner of her apron.

"Don't worry, I'll think of something," said George hopefully. "Have one of these, it'll cheer you up." He passed her the bag of jelly babies. Eave peered inside and her mouth fell open in surprise.

"Fi! Whyfor be yourself givin' us rubber bubbies?" she gasped, prodding them gently. "Oooh ... themselves be most sleepy. Wherefore be the muppy?"

"They haven't got a mummy," laughed George. "They're just sweets." He bit the head off a green one to prove it.

"They taste nice," he said. "Go on, try one."

Eave shook her head.

"Nay, 'tis a shame to be munchin' 'em. Themselves be myne new fambily!" she joked.

While she amused herself making their jelly legs dance along the carved back of the chaise longue, George racked his brains. There must be some other suitable means of transport he could come up with.

"Ah!" he exclaimed. George could have kicked himself – if only he'd thought things through, he could have found a way of sneaking Grandma's wheelchair out of her room. That would have been perfect for Arch to push Granny Cloister in ... but it had gone in the ambulance.

"Ah? Does yourself be havin' a grand plan, Jowge?" asked Eave, hopefully.

"Nope," he confessed sheepishly. "Thought I did for a second. Are you sure there's nothing else with wheels on in this loft that we could use?"

"Nay ... us has a tea trolley," said Lofty. "But itself has oh-nee three wheels and themselves be most wobblee."

A few more moments passed in silence, then Eave looked up from nursing her jelly babies and made an announcement.

"Lo! Myneself has a pushin' chair full of baldy bears in myne boudoir. 'Tis meant for littleys but Grandmuppy Cloister be weighin' no more than a feathie. Herself might fit!"

"'Tis worth a try," agreed Lofty. "Us must be testin' it!" Eave darted off to her bedroom and returned with an old-fashioned pushchair with a canvas seat. It reminded George of a deckchair but it was a reasonable size and although the wheels squeaked, they seemed quite sturdy. Eave parked it and snapped on the brake.

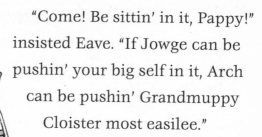

"Come! Be sittin' in it, Pappy!" insisted Eave. "If Jowge can be pushin' your big self in it, Arch can be pushin' Grandmuppy Cloister most easilee."

"Right you are, Littley!" Lofty plonked himself down onto the seat with a broad grin on his face.

"'Tis most comfortiblaaaaagh!" he declared, as the rotten fabric split under his weight and his bottom fell straight through, breaking the rusty catch that secured the folding device. George watched helplessly as the pushchair collapsed and snapped shut with Lofty inside it.

61

"Fi! Myne pushin' chair has swollied Pappy!" squealed Eave, trying desperately not to laugh at the sight of his kicking feet.

"Help!" wailed Lofty. "Myneself be foldee in half!"

Giggling uncontrollably, George and Eave straightened the pushchair out between them and helped Lofty back onto his feet.

"No harm done!" he exclaimed, as if nothing had happened. Eave put her fist in her mouth to try and control her giggles but as Lofty turned round to dust himself down, both she and George noticed

there was a red jelly baby stuck to the back of his trousers, which set them off again, hooting and spluttering until their ribs ached.

"Yay. Darst say myneself be most amusin'," said Lofty, goodheartedly. "But Arch won't be larfin' if himself turns up and us has no coach for Grandmuppy Cloister."

The mood changed immediately. Eave slumped back down on the chaise longue and gazed at George in despair.

"There's always Plan C!" George said brightly. He didn't have a clue what it was, but he was sure if he kept pacing up and down past the portraits of his intrepid ancestors, an idea would eventually come to him. And, mercifully, it did.

"The petrol mower!" he beamed.

There was an old lawnmower with a wide seat in Grandma Peggy's garden behind the shed. He had no idea if it still worked or even how to start it up but Lofty could fix it, surely? He could fix most things. Unfortunately, the lawnmower was far too heavy to bring up to the attic. There was only one thing for it.

"You'll have to come down, Lofty," said George.

Lofty put both fingers in his ears and gave them a good clean in case he'd misheard.

"*Down*, Jowge?"

Lofty hadn't been Down Below since the night he'd first arrived with Eave two years ago. He'd been watching the house for ages and thought Grandma Peggy had left for good, but it had turned out she'd only gone to stay in a nursing home for a while after a spell in hospital.

A month after Lofty and Eave had moved into her attic, Grandma Peggy returned. They were all prepared to move out, afraid she would catch them, but she had never come upstairs. Nor did the neighbour who had popped in to do her shopping, so they had stayed.

"You won't be caught," said George. "Dad and Grandma won't be back from hospital for ages and Mum isn't due home from work for at least two hours."

But Eave wasn't about to let Lofty leave without a fight. "Pappy darst not be goin' Down Below exceptin' on one condition..." she insisted.

"What condition is that?" asked George.

Eave folded her arms in the manner of a girl who was determined to get her own way.

"Myneself be comin' too, Jowge!"

Once Eave had made up her mind, George knew there was no arguing with her.

CHAPTER FIVE

MOWERS AND MAYHEM

Lofty and Eave crept cautiously out of the attic into George's bedroom. The sudden brightness of the late afternoon sun streaming in through the slanted window caused them to have a fit of sneezing. Terrified that they might be caught, they pinched their noses to silence themselves.

"It's OK," George told them. "Don't be scared. There's no one in."

Suitably reassured, Lofty let loose an enormous sneeze, some of which landed on George's bedside lamp.

Togas and Treasure

"Eughh, Pappy!" scolded Eave. "Us cannot be takin' yourself anywhere!"

"Doesn't matter," said George. As he wiped the lamp with a paper tissue, he became aware of a rhythmic squeaking coming from behind him.

"Wheee! Jowge's mattress be most springley!" whooped Eave, who was jumping up and down on his bed with such enthusiasm that her plaits brushed the ceiling.

"Even I'm not allowed to do that," George protested.

It wasn't the first time they'd been in George's bedroom – he'd had to hide them in there once when his dad hired a rat catcher to check out noises he'd heard in the loft. It had been a narrow escape, but George had promised Lofty and Eave that one day they could spend some proper time in there and play with all his games and gadgets. So far it hadn't happened.

Eave ran her fingers over his DVD collection and opened one of the cases.

"What be this, Jowge?"

"It's a DVD. You can watch films on it."

She held the disc up to the light and stared at it. "Fi! 'Tis not happenin'. Wherefor be the fillum?"

George picked up the remote control and opened the drawer of his DVD player. "You have to put the disc in there and the film comes up on the telly."

Eave kicked her legs excitedly. She patted the bed. "Yay! Pappy? Be sittin' down and watchin' the fillum on the glass box."

69

Lofty sat down and gazed at the screen. "Might as well, Littley! Myneself isn't gettin' out much. Whatfor is a fillum, Jowge?"

"You've never seen a film before?" exclaimed George.

Of course they hadn't! They had no electricity in the loft, so no TV, and Goffins daredn't go to the cinema. He let them watch the opening credits of his favourite dinosaur movie, then he stopped the disc. Eave clapped loudly.

"Myneself be lovin' that fillum!" she exclaimed. "Though 'twas most short."

"That wasn't the whole film," said George apologetically, snapping the disc back in its case. He'd have loved to let them sit and watch films with him all afternoon, but there just wasn't time – they had to get the mower going.

"One night, when Mum and Dad go to a party or something, you can sit in my room and we'll have a film night with popcorn and everything."

Eave's eyes lit up. "Did yourself be hearin' that, Pappy? Soontimes, Jowge be fetchin' us poppin' corns!"

"Come on," he said. "Let's get going before anyone comes back."

George noticed that when Lofty and Eave walked down the first two flights of stairs, they trod cautiously, always leading with the same foot, like toddlers. He found it odd, because they were so nimble and fearless out on the roof.

"Myneself hasn't been climbin' down stairs for many winters," admitted Lofty.

"Of course," realized George. "You're not stair-savvy, right?"

"Us needs to be gettin' our stair-legs," puffed Eave, clinging onto the rail.

71

Unable to resist showing off, George slid
the rest of the way down to the hall via the
banister. After his embarrassment about
being scared of heights up in their territory,
it felt good to show them how agile he was
in his own surroundings.

"Jowge be monkey-fit!" gasped Eave.

"Himself be penguin-fast!" applauded
Lofty.

George wasn't sure if being called a
monkey and a penguin were the compliments
he was hoping for – he'd have preferred to be
compared to an eagle or a lion like Arch, but
it seemed he could never compete with Eave's
perfect brother.

Just then, someone pushed some junk
mail through the letterbox with a loud clatter.
Eave froze then shrieked and shot back up
the stairs after Lofty, who had slipped in his
haste and was scrabbling on his hands and
knees in terror.

"Hey," called George. "It's OK, no one's

after you. It's only a leaflet for pizzas." He waited for them to reappear. They were certainly taking their time, so he called again.

"Come on ... you'll be safe. Trust me. I'm a Carruthers."

He heard some muttering and shuffling, then, looking a bit sheepish, Lofty and Eave bumped back down the stairs on their bottoms.

"Us darst not be too carefree," said Lofty apologetically.

George nodded and, holding their hands, led them towards the kitchen. He was going to take them outside via the back door rather than through Grandma Peggy's French windows, but he almost wished he hadn't, because once they spotted the equipment in there, it was all he could do to hurry them along.

"Yay!" cried Eave, parking herself in front of the washing machine and tapping the glass door impatiently. "Shall us be watchin' another fillum?"

"That's not a telly, that's where we wash our clothes," said George. He showed her the soap tray and opened the door.

"We put the washing powder in here, then we put the dirty socks and things in there, then we close the door, press that button and water comes in and washes them."

"Nay!" said Lofty, fiddling excitedly with the controls. Startled by the sudden high pitched whirr, he leaped into George's arms for protection and shoved his fingers in his ears.

"Fi! 'Tis goin' to take off like a hellishcopter! Duck, Littley!"

"It's perfectly harmless. It's only the spin cycle," said George. "It's probably best if you don't fiddle." He stopped the machine and put Lofty back on his feet. Eave crept out from behind the vegetable rack and narrowed her eyes suspiciously at the dishwasher.

75

"Whatfor does this do, Jowge?"

"It washes the dirty dishes," he explained.

Eave frowned deeply, certain that he was making it all up. "Hands is for washin' dishin's, Jowge."

"Not in this house," he said, pulling open the door and showing her the rows of gleaming plates, cups and cutlery. Meanwhile, Lofty, who had now lost his fear of kitchen gadgets, wandered over to the sink and started playing with the mixer taps.

"Hot an' cold!" he exclaimed, letting the water thunder into the sink, splashing himself and the kitchen windows. "'Tis most luxurious."

George had always taken the kitchen taps for granted, but to a Goffin, whose only supply of water came from the water tank and the clouds, it was luxury beyond belief.

"Yay! 'Tis snowin'!" cried Eave. "Howfor does the snow be gettin' indoors?" She'd found the freezer and all the delights it held – lollies, frosty tubs of ice cream, ready meals.

"What be these, Jowge?" she asked, sniffing a stiff cardboard packet.

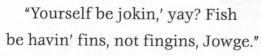

"They're fish fingers."

Eave laughed out loud.

"Yourself be jokin,' yay? Fish be havin' fins, not fingins, Jowge."

There wasn't time to explain – George opened the back door and ushered them out.

"Come on, we have to fix the mower."

Rex, who'd been playing with a stick on the lawn, came bounding up and knocked Eave over.

"Halloo, myne houndbubby!" she squealed as he tried to lick the freckles off her nose.

"Up yourself gets, Littley," said Lofty, helping her to her feet. "Now, wherefor be this mowin' machine, Jowge Carruthers?"

George led Lofty up the garden path and behind the shed.

"There it is!"

Lofty rubbed his hands with glee. He undid the petrol cap and peered down the hole, then he ran his hand over the seat and examined the levers, the brake and the steering wheel.

"Ah... 'Tis a grandly motor and nay mistake!" he said, pulling his spanner out of his jacket pocket and giving the mower a good tweaking.

George squeezed in beside him – there was room for two, especially as one of them was a Goffin.

"Do you think you can get it going, Lofty?"

"Pappy be gettin' anythin' goin'," insisted Eave, who now had Rex in her arms.

Lofty pulled out his handkerchief and wiped a bit of wiring he'd found poking out of the controls.

"All herself be needin' is a tinkerin' and a drink. Be there a can of motor juice in yonder shed, Jowge?"

George went to look. He knew there was a red can of something in the shed – hopefully it was full of petrol. He handed it to Lofty who gave it a sniff, smiled hugely and poured it into the mower tank. He pulled the cord on the starter motor. Nothing happened.

"Oh no, now what?" groaned George.

"Us yanks it harder!" grunted Lofty.

He gave another couple of pulls and the motor puttered into life. Grinning from ear to ear, Lofty took off the brake and began to steer the lawnmower slowly across the grass, cutting a neat swathe as he did so.

"Yay!" cried Eave. "Can myneself be havin' a go?"

"Bide a-while, Littley. Let Pappy be testin' herself!" commanded Lofty, disappearing happily into the orchard with no intention of giving up his seat so soon. Eave followed in his wake, begging to be allowed to drive.

"Pappy! Be givin' myneself a go *now*!"

"Oh, leave him for a bit," smiled George, watching as Lofty merrily circled the apple trees. "He's enjoying himself."

Truly, Lofty hadn't looked so happy in ages. Eave held back and watched him too, plucking a ripe apple and biting into it noisily.

"Isn't yourself gaggin' to drive?" she asked George.

Of course he was, but after he'd crashed the Goff-cart, he didn't dare, in case something went wrong. Lofty finished a few more circuits of the orchard, then came back before George could answer.

"Herself be drivin' like a dream," he said, jumping down. "Your turn, myne Littley."

81

It was too high for Eave to climb in without a leg-up, so she tucked her full skirt into her bloomers and George obliged.

"You do know what you're doing, don't you?" he asked as she took the wheel.

"Oh, Jowge, yourself be such a fussin' pot," she scolded, setting off past the runner beans. George followed behind, but as she went past the vegetable patch, she sped up and he had to run to keep up.

"Eave, slow down," he panted.

As she hit the slope leading to the fish pond, her expression changed.

"Myneself can't be slowin' down. Myneself cannot be reachin' the foot pedil!"

George tried to jump in beside her to seize the controls, but it was too late – with an almighty splash, Eave and the mower drove straight into the pond.

"Alack!" cried Lofty. "Myne mower be a-drownin'!"

"Never mind your mower, *myneself* be a-drownin'!" wailed Eave as the water rushed over her lap.

Plan C had failed miserably and as George waded in and carried her to safety, he was really struggling to stay cheerful.

"Oh, Jowge, yourself be hippo-strong!" swooned Eave as she lay soggily in his arms. Not ox-strong, he noted, like Arch. It didn't feel like much of a compliment.

"I'm a hippo? Thanks a lot," muttered George.

"But Jowge, hippopottimouths be myne favourite beasts," she reassured him. "Themselves be most fearless. Most tough. Most ... hamsom!"

She gazed at him with such admiration, George couldn't help feeling good about himself. No one had ever called him handsome before. He tossed his head back in what he hoped was a manly way and was just about to plonk Eave down on the grass when the doorbell rang.

His heart leapt into his mouth. What if his Mum had come home early and forgotten her key? It wouldn't be the first time. He ran towards the house with Eave in his arms.

"Alack!" panicked Lofty, running in desperate circles. "Us will be cotched! Wherefor will us hide?"

George lifted the iron handle on the lid of big concrete shelter where Grandma Peggy used to keep her fuel for the fire. The inside was black with coal dust and full of spiders.

"Quick!" he hissed. "Both of you, get in the coal bunker!"

"Myneself be – uff – uff – soggy and afrit!" whimpered Eave as she scrambled onto the bunker and dropped down through the small, square hole after her father.

"Just don't make a sound," begged George.

He slammed the lid back on and ran inside to see who was at the door.

CHAPTER SIX

SOOT AND SCOOTERS

To George's enormous relief, it wasn't his mother at the front door. It was a delivery man in a flat cap holding a clip board.

"Mrs Peggy Carruthers?" he said.

"No, I'm George."

The delivery man jabbed his biro in the direction of the house.

"This is the *residence* of Mrs Peggy Carruthers, is it? Only I've got her Freedom Excel Mobility Scooter in the back of my van. Should have delivered it last week, only there was a strike at the scooter factory. These things happen." He tapped his foot impatiently and peered over George's head.

"Is Mrs Carruthers in, only she needs to sign for it."

George shook his head. "Grandma Peggy's gone to hospital."

"Well, it needs to be signed for by a responsible adult – is your old man in?"

"My old man? Oh, you mean Dad?"

George was about to say no, but then he changed his mind. He'd just had an idea.

"Yeah, yeah, my dad is in... Don't go! I'll fetch him."

George ran back through the house and into the garden. He lifted the lid off the coal bunker and spoke into the black hole.

Two pairs of bright green eyes stared back at him.

"Hey, Eave, I'll be back for you in a sec. Lofty? Come out! I need you to pretend to be my dad..."

Lofty held up his grimy hand and George grabbed it and helped him back up through the hole. He was absolutely filthy – his skin was blackened with soot, his hair was covered in sticky grey cobwebs, and there was a spider hanging off his ear. George flicked it away.

"There's a man at the door," he explained rapidly. "He's delivering a brand new scooter for Grandma but he needs a grown-up to sign for it or he'll take it away and we can't let him do that."

"Whyfor can't us?" asked Lofty, scratching his sooty scalp in bemusement.

"Don't you see?" whispered George excitedly. "That scooter is the answer to Granny Cloister's prayers. If we play our cards right, Arch can pick it up tonight and drive it off."

Lofty looked even more confused. "Play us cards, Jowge?"

There was no time to go into details. "Trust me," said George. "All you have to do is sign the delivery note and we're away!"

Lofty was understandably anxious. Apart from George, he'd never come face to face with a non-Goffin in all his life. Before they went into the hall, he grabbed the back of George's hoody.

"Jowge! Whatfor must myneself be scribblin' on yonder dockyment?"

"P. Carruthers. Just do a squiggly line."

Lofty followed him through the kitchen, leaving black footprints all over the tiles. He hesitated at the door that led into the hallway.

"Jowge? Must myneself be sayin' halloo?"

"Let me do the talking," insisted George. "Don't you say a word."

The delivery man was looking at his watch as they returned as if to make the point that his time was far more precious than theirs, but when he looked up and saw Lofty in his blackened smoking jacket and his crazy hair full of coal dust, he almost fell off the step.

"Mr... Carruthers?" he sputtered.

"Yes, this is Dad," said George. "Sorry for the delay, Dad's been ... um ... practising his sooty clown routine. He belongs to a circus, don't you, Dad?"

Lofty looked up at the delivery man and smiled earnestly.

"Yay!" he said, wiping his face on his sleeve. "Myneself be a most hilarious circuss genteelmen."

George glared at him. Remembering far too late that he wasn't supposed to speak, Lofty clapped his hands over his mouth and stared at his shoes.

"Dad's from Norway," laughed George nervously. "That's why he talks funny – they all talk like that at the Norwegian circus."

The delivery man didn't look convinced but even so, he thrust the clipboard with the docket into Lofty's hands and pointed to the dotted line where he was meant to sign. Lofty took the biro and, with shaking fingers, he did the deed.

The delivery man didn't give the signature a second glance – he was in a tearing hurry – and in no time at all, he'd lowered the shiny red scooter off the van.

"It's all ready to go – should do about
thirty miles before you need to recharge
the battery. Where d'you want it, mate?"

He looked to Lofty
for the answer.

Knowing he wasn't to utter a sound,
Lofty gazed helplessly at George who
came to the rescue by striding over to the
garage.

"It's alright, I'll open it for you ... Dad," he
insisted, raising the door. "You go inside and
get back to your hilarious Norwegian clown
routine."

93

George ushered Lofty inside and half-closed the front door. He was anxious to get him out of sight in case one or both of his parents returned and found him on the doorstep. He'd been keeping an eye out for them all the while and was beginning to lose his nerve.

As the delivery man rolled the Freedom Excel Scooter into the garage and handed him the manual and the keys, George felt that, for once, fate had smiled upon him. Even Arch couldn't fail to be impressed by this vehicle, surely?

It was safe, it was fast and it was good-looking. It had a padded leather seat and a horn, which would certainly come in handy when Arch drove it off-road, if any badgers got in his way. George was dying to parp it but managed to control the urge.

Closing the garage door behind him, he noted that the scooter even had a generous wire basket on the front for Granny Cloister to put her suitcase in. Arch could drive it to Great Uncle Garrat's overnight and return it before the rest of the house was awake. Grandma Peggy need never know it had gone missing.

Feeling very pleased with himself, George explained all this to Lofty and Eave as he chivvied them back up into the attic. Eave was fussing about her dirty clothes.

"Fi! Myneself will never be gettin' em clean, no matter how much scrubbin'." She had to wash everything by hand in the attic. It was hard work – George had seen her do it and he felt rather guilty because it made her little fingers red raw.

Togas and Treasure

"I'll take them to the launderette for you, I promise," he said. It would of course be easier to put Eave's clothes in the washing machine, but say he accidentally left a pair of her of her frilly bloomin's, as she called them, in there – how could he explain that away to his mother?

It was bad enough trying to explain things a few minutes later when his parents came home with Grandma, and demanded to know why there was soot everywhere.

"It was Rex," lied George. "I took him for a walk and he rolled in some ash. I've bathed him but I didn't have time to clean the house because I had a bit of an accident and then I had to do my Roman project."

"What sort of accident? Are you hurt?" asked his mother. She still had her nurse's uniform on and instinctively began to examine him for injuries. She felt the cuffs of his tracksuit bottoms. They were soaking. He hadn't had time to change.

"Why are your trouser legs wet?" she asked. "Did you get caught short?"

"No!" he said. "I haven't wet myself! It happened when I was mowing the lawn."

"What happened?" snapped his father. "What have you done to the mower?"

"I haven't *done* anything to it. It just fell in the pond," confessed George.

Grandma sat down heavily on a kitchen chair. "Isn't anyone going to ask how I am?" she grumped.

"How are you, Grandma?" asked George, happy to change the subject.

George's dad looked out of the kitchen window in disbelief. "How did the mower fall in the pond?" he demanded.

"I was only trying to be helpful," said George. "Mum keeps asking you to cut the lawn and you're always too busy so I thought I'd fix the mower and do it for you."

"That was decent of him, wasn't it Phillip?" said Grandma Peggy. "Pity about your driving though, boy. That's two prangs in one day, isn't it?"

"At least no one was hurt," said George's mum, trying to diffuse the situation. "Why don't you put the car in the garage, Phil? I'll make us all a cup of tea."

"About time too. I'm parched," muttered
Grandma. "Got any decent biscuits?"

George sat down at the kitchen table
next to her and whispered in her
ear. "You've had
a delivery."

Grandma raised her eyebrows then hastily
put her finger to her lips. "Don't tell him.
Don't tell your father. Probably not a good
time now."

Grandma was right about that. When
George's father returned, he was sucking
his cheeks in and out in the way that he did
when he was trying not to lose his temper.

"Whose is that mobility scooter in the garage?" he asked, trying to catch Grandma's eye. Grandma dunked a custard cream into her tea and refused to look at him.

"What business is it of yours?" she said airily.

An argument broke out – at least that's how it sounded to George. His dad insisted there was no argument; he was just trying to look after Grandma and, in his opinion, it wasn't safe for her to be driving that scooter about at her age.

"You should never have bought it without consulting me," he said.

Grandma Peggy rapped her teaspoon on the table. "I shall do as I please in my own house. I'm your mother!" she reminded him.

To George's dismay, his father refused to back down.

"It's going back tonight, Mum. Be sensible. Will you call the company or shall I?"

His dad picked up the phone. George looked at the clock. Arch would be here in five hours.

But would the scooter?

CHAPTER SEVEN

CODES AND CASSOCKS

George went to his room. The hoo-ha over
the new scooter was in full swing downstairs.
Whether or not the delivery man would come
and collect it tonight, he still didn't know.
He felt angry with his dad: how dare he tell
Grandma what to do?

   He knew how it felt. Apart from Lofty,
adults were always telling him what to do.
Everyone who was older than him seemed to
think they had a right to boss him about. OK,
so he was still a kid, but Grandma was eighty!
How old did you have to be before you were
allowed to do as you pleased?

He flopped onto his bed. His head was spinning. If the scooter was taken away, maybe he could still sneak Grandma's wheelchair out and give that to Arch. But how? It was one thing to creep into her bedroom and remove a tea tray, but how was he supposed to wheel the chair out without waking her? He was in half a mind to go back downstairs and ask Grandma outright if he could borrow it; she'd want to know why, but he could surely think of some good excuse.

But, the more he tried, the harder it was to think of one. Maybe he could say he needed to draw a wheelchair for his art homework; but then why would he need to take it from her room? Maybe he could pretend he needed it to take his 'friend' Hans Lofthausen to a football match because Hans had a broken leg. But Grandma knew George never went to football matches, especially not at this time of day.

George was getting more desperate by the minute. Maybe he should just break the promise he'd made to Lofty and Eave and tell Grandma that Eave's brother needed to borrow the wheelchair to shift his Granny. It could be their little secret. He got off the bed and went out of his bedroom door. He stood at the top of the stairs, then he turned back round. No, no, no. He couldn't bring himself to break Lofty and Eave's trust.

Totally defeated, he lay back down on his bed, wondering how on earth he was going to confess to Lofty that his plans had fallen through and that Arch would have to go home empty-handed. With his stomach in knots, George somehow drifted off to sleep.

He was woken mid-dream by the sound of an owl hooting. He sat up with a start and rubbed his eyes. What time was it? It was dark outside and he was in his pyjamas, which was odd, because he was certain he'd nodded off in his dayclothes, and they were now neatly stacked on a chair. His mum must have come to say goodnight, found him asleep and dressed him for bed. The owl hooted again.

George leapt up, his hair standing on end. That was no owl ... that was the sound of someone imitating an owl cry on a twigaloo! The only people who played twigaloos were Goffins. It could mean only one thing: Arch was Down Below!

George tiptoed down the first flight of stairs. Had his parents gone to bed? He listened at their door. The light was out and he could hear his father snoring. Even so, his mother was a light sleeper. He mustn't tread on the creaky stair. He slid down the banisters and went into the kitchen, hoping that Rex was asleep.

As soon as George opened the door, Rex whimpered with delight to see his master at this strange hour, and leapt out of his basket.

"Shh, Rex. Good boy. Look ... biscuits!"

George filled the dog bowl. If Rex was eating, he wouldn't bark. Rex, delighted to be offered breakfast so shortly after dinner, began to tuck in. With Rex distracted, George picked up the garage keys from the saucer on the windowsill, unbolted the back door as quietly as he could, and crept out into the garden.

He peered down the side of the house. Under the moonlight, he could just about make out a small, shadowy figure leaning against the far end wall. He coughed softly to catch his attention.

"Arch?"

The figure turned and walked silently towards him, his gooseberry-green eyes illuminating the darkness like traffic lights.

"Halloo, Jowge."

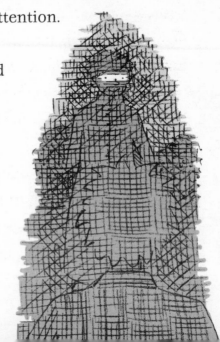

Arch was much shorter than George had
expected but quite well built. He pushed back
his red hair, which had been oiled into a quiff,
then he drew himself up to his full height and
whispered in George's ear.

"Wherefor be the cart?"

"There's been a slight change of plan,"
admitted George, trying to calm his voice.
Was the scooter still in the garage? He
crossed his fingers. Surely he'd have heard
the van and rumpus if the delivery man had
come and taken it; Grandma Peggy wouldn't

have let it go without a fight. But what if the scooter had gone and he'd slept through it all? He couldn't put it off any longer. He'd have to go and check.

"Wait for me round the back, Arch," he said.

George tiptoed towards the front of the house. Making sure that the curtains at his parents' bedroom window were closed, he opened the garage door as quietly as possible, hanging onto the edge so that the hinges wouldn't squeak. He held his breath and peered inside.

The scooter was still there! George had to bite his own tongue to stop himself whooping with joy. But his dad had parked the car next to it so tightly, there was hardly a coat of paint between them. He grabbed the scooter by the handlebars, took off the brake and, with some difficulty, steered it past the wing mirror of the Renault, cringing as a faint line of white appeared on the scooter where the bodywork scratched the wall.

Togas and Treasure

Having wrestled it onto the drive, he closed the garage door and pushed the Freedom Excel down the side of the house towards the back garden. It would be much safer for Arch to leave from there rather than the front. There was a gate at the end of Grandma Peggy's orchard, which led to a country lane. At this time of night, Arch could ride across the lane and through the spinney opposite without fear of bumping into anyone.

George's triumphant arrival with the scooter wasn't greeted with the enthusiasm he'd expected, but this was only because Arch was otherwise occupied. He had his torch out and was using it to flash messages to Lofty and Eave in Morse code.

George knew what Morse
code was because his father
had been a boy scout and
had often bored him with
tales of how he and his mate
Bavin Bannerjee had had to
communicate with torches on
camping trips to Wales. Now George
wished he'd paid more attention so
he could translate the conversation
the Goffins were having. He wondered
if they were saying anything about him.

Arch was aware of George but he
didn't turn to look at him. He was too
busy de-coding the message that Eave
was sending back to him.

"Myne oh-nee sister!" he sighed. "Us
be missing yourself most terribil, too."

He blew a kiss in her direction. If any
other boy had blown his sister a kiss – his
old mate Warren, for example – George
would have gagged and thought it was soppy.

He didn't feel that way about Arch though. Now that he'd actually met him, he realized that Arch was neither pompous nor a threat. In fact, he was modest, gentle, almost shy.

George wanted to comfort him, to reassure him that he'd been taking great care of his sister and dad and always would. Knowing that Lofty and Eave were so near, yet knowing that he couldn't visit them must have been awfully hard for Arch to bear, even if he was lionbrave. George could understand that.

He watched quietly as Arch stared longingly up at the roof. He cut a striking figure in his billowing cassock that his mother, Ariel, must have shortened from an original. George imagined it had once belonged to a bell-ringer who'd left it in the belfry of the church long before Granny Cloister moved in.

As the moon went behind a cloud, Arch put his torch away and turned round. When he saw the scooter, his face split into a warm smile, like a toasted croissant.

"Will it do?" asked George, in what he hoped was a masculine way but, to his shame, came out rather squeaky.

"Do?" exclaimed Arch. "Jowge, 'twill do most royal!"

To George's huge relief, Arch's voice was just as squeaky as his and when Arch clapped him on the back and called him his 'oh-nee step-in brother', George felt that they had truly bonded.

George had always wanted a brother. In the past, when Eave had bragged that Arch was the best brother anyone could have, George had felt really jealous. But now that he'd met him, he knew she wasn't exaggerating.

He didn't want Arch to leave. He fantasized about the games of cricket they could play together in the summer. The football matches in winter. Maybe they could even go fishing. But if you were friends with a Goffin it had to be in secret, no matter how hard that was. George promised himself that one day, he would find a way to bring the Goffins back together, even if it was just for one glorious afternoon.

George helped Arch push the scooter to the bottom of the orchard. He laughed softly when he saw the petrol mower up to its waist in water in the middle of the pond.

"Whatfor be itself doin' in there?" he asked.

"It's a long story," grinned George. "I'll tell you sometime."

When they were out of earshot, Arch climbed onto the scooter seat and turned the key in the ignition. As the engine ticked over, he turned to George and nodded gratefully.

"Yourself be doin' myne fambily a normous Kindness. Thanklee, bro."

"Don't mention it," said George.

Arch reached inside his cassock and handed him a small parcel, wrapped in a silk hanky.

"For Eave," he said. "Be givin' her myne besterly love, yay?"

George put it in his pocket. "I will. You'll bring the scooter back at dawn, won't you?"

Arch nodded. "Don't be waitin' up, Jowge. Myneself will be parkin' it afore sunrise."

George opened the gate. Arch drove forward but just before he shot off into the night, he eased off the accelerator and glanced over his shoulder.

"Jowge, is yourself wantin' to come for the ride?"

George wanted to. He wanted to go with Arch and meet Ariel and Granny Cloister more than anything, but something stopped him. What was it, had he no sense of adventure? Was he a coward, scared his dad would find out and tell him off? No, it wasn't that.

Arch was on a mission. He was in a hurry – and George didn't want to do everything in a rush. It would spoil things. He'd rather wait for a night when they could enjoy themselves properly without having to worry about their grandmothers.

"Another time, Arch," he said. "I need to make sure everything goes to plan here."

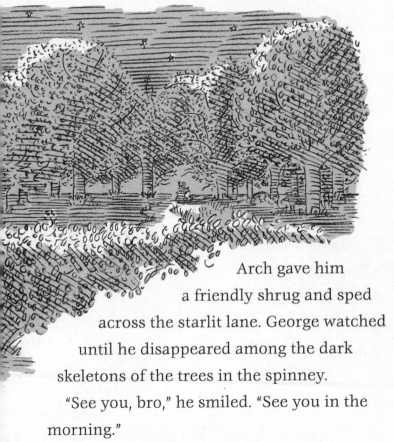

Arch gave him a friendly shrug and sped across the starlit lane. George watched until he disappeared among the dark skeletons of the trees in the spinney.

"See you, bro," he smiled. "See you in the morning."

There was no way George was going to sleep tonight.

CHAPTER EIGHT

TOGAS AND TREASURE

The night air was damp. George shivered as he made his way back across the garden.

He wasn't in the slightest bit sleepy though. He was buzzing and so was Eave, he discovered when he went up to the attic to see the Goffins. She couldn't stop talking.

"Jowge? Did myne Arch be lovin' the scooter? Himself be lookin' well, yay? Did himself be guessin' how long themselves will be takin' to get to Great Uncool Garrat's?"

She didn't give George a chance to answer any of her questions. "Did yourself be likin' myne brother Arch?" she continued. "Did

119

himself be givin' myneself a gift?" She began to frisk George vigorously, checking inside his hood and feeling his pockets.

"Now, Littley!" said Lofty. "Be-calm yourself. Be leavin' poor Jowge be!"

"It's OK," laughed George. "Eave, shut your eyes and hold out your hands."

She looked at him curiously. "Whyfor, Jowge?"

"It'll add to the surprise."

"Oh... Welly well."

She squeezed her eyelids shut and stretched her arms out in front of her expectantly. George took Arch's gift out of his pocket and put it into her cupped palms. He was as excited as she was to see what was inside the mysterious silk hanky. It felt quite heavy.

"Can myneself be lookin' now?" asked Eave.

"Yep."

She felt the little parcel in her fingers and struggled to undo the knot in the handkerchief.

"Let Pappy be helpin'," offered Lofty. "Arch be tyin' most complicockled knots."

"Nay! Myneself be doin' it!" insisted Eave, twisting her body away so that she could get first glimpse.

"What is it?" asked George.

"'Tis treasure!" gasped Eave. She held it up to the candlelight. "'Tis most rare and sparklin'! Please be claspin' it round myneself, Jowge."

It was a very old locket encrusted with emeralds and pearls.

"Wow! Are those stones real?" exclaimed George.

She lifted up her wild mane of copper hair, exposing her tiny white neck. George held the necklace by the clasps and draped it round her throat.

Togas and Treasure

"'Tis a most pretty piece!" announced Lofty. "Darst say 'twas crafted by Ancient Roamins. Most likelee Arch be findin' it buried afore the olden-day diggers be arrivin'."

He hunted in his pockets for the old monocle lens he used to examine precious objects, but it was in his other jacket; he'd had to change out of his green quilted one after it had got so dirty in the coal bunker. Both he and Eave had tried to brush the coal dust out of their hair but their faces were still smudgy.

"Myneself has a magifryin' lens someplace..." muttered Lofty, and he wandered off to find it.

"Us has a book about Ancient Roamins. Maybe itself be tellin' about myne treasure!" said Eave.

She followed Lofty into their sitting room and while he looked for the magnifying glass, she searched through the heavy oak bookcase and found the history book. She curled up on the faded lilac chaise longue and flicked through the pages.

"Come see, Jowge," she said.

He sat down and looked at the pictures over her shoulder. "Can I borrow this for my school project? I haven't even started it yet," he groaned.

"Myneself be dreamin' of lessins at school," said Eave wistfully. "Yourself be most luckee to have teachin' and learnin' and larks with friends, Jowge."

It had never occurred to George that he was lucky to go to school, especially not first thing on a Monday. But when he thought about it, even if he didn't always enjoy lessons, he wouldn't want to grow up without being

123

able to read, write or know all the stuff you needed to know to get on in life. And even though he didn't have a best friend yet, his class mates were good fun. He was giggling to himself about his pretend friend Hans when Eave interrupted his flow of thought.

"Ooh, this scribblin' does say that Ancient Roamins be wearin' togas and havin' normous feasts an'..."

She stopped mid-speech and grabbed George's elbow. "Jowge ... *us* could be havin' a normous Roamin' feast!" She snapped the book shut. "Us has meaty paste and biskies and jellybubbies, yay? Us must be dressin' in togas and loungin' in us roof garden and feastin' til dawn! Come, Jowgey!"

She took his hand and ran with him down the corridor of antique mirrors. He stooped down and went through the door of the grandfather clock into her bedroom.

"Be pullin' off the beddin'!" she whooped, whisking the eiderdown off with all the

teddies and old dolls that she'd tipped out of
the pushchair earlier.

George was confused. "Eave, what are you—"

She grabbed the top sheet and wound it
around herself. "Makin' myneself a Roamin'
toga ... itself oh-nee needs pinnin'."

She rooted round in her dressing table
drawer and held up an enamel brooch shaped
like a pansy, and a kilt pin.

"Which one
will yourself
be wearin',
Jowge?"

"Erm ... you have the pansy," he said hastily. He dragged the bottom sheet off her bed and allowed her to wind it round him.

"Be liftin' your arms, Jowgie. Nay wrigglin'!"

He told himself he should feel foolish, playing dressing-up with a nine year old girl, but he didn't. Maybe it was because he was high on lack of sleep; maybe it was because he wanted to please Eave. Or maybe it was because he'd never had anyone to play with when he was little. Whatever the reason, he didn't care. He just felt happy.

"Hail Caesar!" he laughed, looking at himself in the mirror.

"Halloo too, Brutus!" said Eave, grabbing the eiderdown. "Us will be lyin' on this under the stars, yay?"

They fetched the food George had brought, put it on a tray and climbed out of the skylight onto the roof garden. It was bright with candles flickering in assorted jars.

"Oh, 'tis magical!" gasped Eave.

Lofty must have gone out ahead of them and lit them as a surprise. George clung to the washing line to steady himself while Eave skipped about searching for Lofty.

"Pappy? Be showin' yourself."

He stepped out from behind the chimney stack. "'Tis a most rare occasion," he said, helping her to spread out the eiderdown. "To see myne Arch be makin' myneself as happy as a hog in a honneepot."

He took a swig of the dandelion and burdock that George had provided, but having never tried it before, he hadn't realized it was fizzy and the expression on his face was priceless.

"Alack! Myne hooter be burstin' with bubbils!" he snorted.

127

Togas and Treasure

By the time they'd buttered the biscuits and eaten the whole packet along with the cucumber, meat paste, yogurt and jelly babies, George felt stuffed. He lay back on the eiderdown and, for the first time ever, he didn't care if he fell off the roof or not. He too was as happy as a hog in a honey pot and there he lay until just before dawn, when the soft purring of the scooter alerted him to Arch's arrival.

By the time George had managed to get downstairs and back into the garden, Arch had already put the scooter back in the garage and was loitering near Grandma Peggy's French windows. George wasn't about to let him go without saying goodbye.

"Psst... Arch! Did your mum and gran make it to the windmill OK?"

Arch, looking somewhat surprised to see him, gave him the thumbs-up. "Myne fambily be giftin' yourself this..." said Arch, taking something off the bird table. "Pappy was to hook it afore sunrise, but yourself be awake already!"

"Couldn't sleep," said George, feeling somewhat self-conscious in his toga.

Arch handed him a bright, metal object. "For myne step-in brother," he said. "Yourself be myne hero."

Togas and Treasure

It was a medal. A Roman medal! It could have been that he'd eaten too many jelly babies, but George felt himself swelling with

pride. He gave Arch the sherbet fountain. He was afraid it wasn't a fair swap for the medal, but Arch accepted it with grace, and was fascinated by the liquorice pipe sticking out of the top.

"You're meant to suck the sherbet up through it," explained George.

Arch frowned in concentration but when the fizzy powder hit his tongue, his eyebrows almost shot under his quiff. He shook his head like a dog with wet fur and beamed at George.

"Whoah... Thanklee, bro! This sherbit is buzzin'!"

Above Arch's head, George could see a golden halo: the sun was rising. It was time to go.

"Come back soon," he said to Arch as he waved goodbye. "I'll think of a way of getting us all together. Your sister and your dad – they really miss you."

George was going to miss him too. He watched wistfully until Arch disappeared into the sunrise, then he crept back upstairs to his bedroom, pinned the medal to his pyjamas and dreamed about Romans, windmills and hogs until he was rudely awoken by lots of shouting. He threw his dressing gown on and went downstairs to investigate.

His family were all sitting round the kitchen table looking extremely agitated, except for Grandma Peggy, who looked as if she was rather enjoying herself. George grabbed himself a chair.

"What's up, dad?"

According to his father, he'd just been outside to clean the car only to find that the garage door was unlocked and that someone had taken Grandma Peggy's new scooter for a joyride.

"Oh, no. Did they put it back?" asked George, trying to keep a straight face.

His father nodded. "The trouble is, it's covered in mud and it's got a scratch on one side..."

"Which means he can't send it back!" hooted Grandma, slapping her thigh.

No wonder she looked so pleased.

"Fantastic!" he said, high-fiving her. "You go, Grandma!"

George's dad glared at them both.

"You two seem as thick as thieves," he muttered suspiciously. "You didn't take that scooter for a drive by any chance, did you son?"

Grandma threw back her head and snickered like a horse. "*Him?* It can't have been him, Phillip! He's already written off a go-cart and a lawnmower. He can't drive to save his life, can you, boy?"

"No, Grandma," agreed George.

But he knew a boy who could.

Goffin Dictionary

A

a-blowin' blow, as in wind
accibump accident
afrit scared
a-loney lonely
afore before
alack oh dear, alas
aloft above
amberlance ambulance
appil apple

B

be-accidents by accident
be-fall drop off, fall off
be-fallen fallen off
be-fetch retrieve, go and fetch
be-fix fix an item to something
be-guise disguise
be-morn in the morning
be-nights tonight, at night
be-scribe write
be-snuff snuff out
be-thunk thought
be-wilbered bewildered
be-yondertimes later on
besterly very best
betterly better than
bicycool bicycle
bide wait
binockles binoculars
biskies biscuits
bittilee bitterly
betwixt between
blam to hit hard
blankin's blankets
blisful lovely
bloomin's knickers/underwear
boggyman bogeyman

bomb-fired blown up, as with a bomb
borned to be born
botticks bottom
bottils bottles
boudoir bedroom
bubbils bubbles
bubby baby
bulltough strong
butteries batteries
buttyfly butterfly
brainhat helmet
breakfeast breakfast
broilin' boiling

C

candils candles
carefree relaxed
chamber room
charitee kindness
cheery cherry
chickeree chicory
chimbley chimney, also name of Eave's pet pigeon
chimbley egg pigeon's egg

choclick chocolate
choon tune or song
chrizzled christened
clamber climb
clangerin' making a noise
closet toilet
clucky egg hen's egg
cockerill cockerel
coddle cuddle
cometh is coming, has come
comftible comfortable
complicockled complicated
cotch, cotched catch, caught
cottin cotton
crafts skills
creepin' crawlin's insects, invertebrates
crewilly cruely
crockydile crocodile
crumpilled crumpled

Goffin Dictionary

D

dandyloon dandelion
darst not dare not
deaded killed
deadilly dangerous
demolishin' man
demolition man
dentipeep dentist
dishin's dishes
dinnin's dinner
do-long year all year
dockyments documents
does do
doin's bodily waste
dread fear – also dreadfill
dressin' maker dressmaker
drownded drowned

E

ebidle edible
eekwill equal
endelong lengthways
evertimes forever

f

fambily family
fearfill scared
feathies feathers

fi! exclamation of fear, help!
fillum film
fluttermouse pipistrelle bat
foul horrid
foxsharp wily
frizzled fried
fruitibles fruit

G

gargled strangled
genteelman gentleman
ghoost ghost
gnits gnats
goblit fancy cup
Goff-cart go-cart
Goffin race of people from
Inish Goff, now sunk in the
Irish Sea
goggils glasses
goobies gooseberries
goodly great, marvellous

grandmuppy grandma
grandpappy grandfather
grandplods grandparents
gratefill grateful
grinnin' taking the mick
grisly horrible

H

halloo hello
hamsom handsome
hanglebars handlebars
hark listen
has have
hastilee quickly
hath it has
haul a fishing catch, as in a haul of bird bread
head ouch headache
healthee healthy
heartilee heartily
hellishcopter hellicopter

himself he
hippopottimouth hippopotamus
hither here, as in come hither
honnee honey
hook take, steal
horse sittle saddle
horse tack bridle etc
houndbubby puppy
hounds dogs
howfor? how can we therefore?
hundrid one hundred

I

iggerant ignorant

J

jerkilee in a jerky manner
Jowge George
joyfill joyful

Goffin Dictionary

K

knickybockers bloomers

L

langwidge language
larfin' make fun of
larkswift swift as a lark
laydee woman
leaf sweat condensation, dew
lemmin'aid lemonade
lessins lessons
lionbrave fearless
littley child, kid
lo! behold
long-a-long very long
Lundiner born in London
lurgies disease

M

magifryin' magnifying
marbils marbles
meatypaste meat paste
merrilee happily
merrimakin' having fun
middil middle
mischeef trouble
miseree misery
moffs moths

morn morning
most very
motor car
munnee money
muppy mum
myne mine, belonging to me
myneself me, I

N

nakey without clothing
nay no
neighblies neighbours
neighbourly from the neighbourhood
newspapey newspaper
niddle needle
nightlie nightie
nightly at night time
normous enormous
nutriments nourishing food

O

oh-nee only, if only
olde old
olden-day diggers archaeologist
once-a-time once
owlwise intelligent
ox-strong very strong
oziz ounces

P

pappy dad
parlour lounge
parrit parrot
peacefill peaceful
peacefun peaceful and harmless
pedil pedal
peek look, observe, study
peepil people
per-lum plum
piggy toe
pilloows pillows
plummet to fall
plumptious plump
plush soft
ponky smelly
'poon harpoon

poppin' corns popcorn
pricklepig hedgehog

Q

R

raidi-who radio
rare unusual, unlikely
rarin' urgent desire to do something now
redded embarrassed
rellies relatives
riled angry
rillytruly to tell the truth
Roamin Roman
roly-round tied
roof-fish to fish from the roof for food or items
roof legs to have no fear of heights
rumpus noise

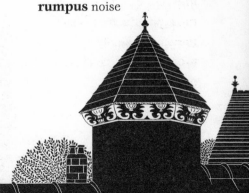

Goffin Dictionary

S

sammidge sandwich

sandils sandles

sausagins sausages

scarifyin' scare

screak squeak, scrape

scribblin's written matter, documents

serpent snake

shouldies shoulders

sicklee ill

skrike shriek

sky-dizzy afraid of heights

sky-like skylight

sky-savvy to know how to move around a roof safely

slew kill

slippins slippers

smincey little, small amount

sniff an odour

snitch nose

sockets socks

softlee quietly

somebiddy somebody, usually a woman

sorely painful

sorrowfill sorry

spewerpipe sewer

spookfill spooky

springly springy

squill squirrel

squish squash

step-in sister/brother substitute sister/brother

sunsit sunset

swede suede

sweetyheart girlfriend/ boyfriend

swiftlee quickly

swollied swallowed

T

tastefill delicious

thanklee thank you

thus that is why, therefore

tiddlypoles tadpoles

'tis it is

to-gathered together

trash and hide to disarrange a place and remove traces of habitation

travellin' be-foots walking

trove treasured junk

trubbil trouble

'twas it was

U

uncool uncle
us we
usefil useful

V

veggibles vegetables
vessels pots etc
villins baddies

W

walligator alligator
welly well very well
whiff to detect a smell
whumperin' whimpering
whyfor why
windyfone gramophone
wobbilin' wobbling
woe misery
Worldly War One WWI
Worldly War Two WWII
wringle mangle

wristit bracelet
wype to wipe

X

Y

yalp yelp
yay yes
yearnin' hoping
yesternights last night
yestertimes yesterday or in the past
yuletime winter
yonder over there
yourself you

Z

Don't miss the Goffins' other adventures!

Is there a Goffin in your attic?